TAZ'S GROSS RIDDLES

ILLUSTRATED BY J.T. MCKINSEY

A GOLDEN BOOK • NEW YORK

WESTERN PUBLISHING COMPANY, INC., RACINE, WISCONSIN 53404

WHY DID TAZ EAT A BUCKET OF TERMITES?

THE BUCKET OF TOOTHPICKS HE ATE GAVE HIM INDIGESTION.

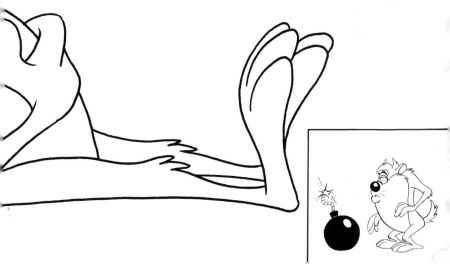

WHY DID TAZ PUT WORMS IN HIS PEANUT BUTTER AND JELLY SANDWICH?

BECAUSE CATERPILLARS ARE TOO CRUNCHY.

WHY DID TAZ CROSS THE ROAD?

TO GET TO THE GARBAGE TRUCK PARKED ON THE OTHER SIDE.

WHY DID TAZ EAT A BOWL OF LIVE CATERPILLARS?

HE WANTED TO HAVE BUTTERFLIES IN HIS STOMACH.

WHY DID TAZ EAT ONE HUNDRED
100-WATT BULBS?

HIS DOCTOR TOLD HIM TO LIGHTEN
UP HIS DIET.

WHAT ARE SWEET AND TAKE A LONG TIME TO GET TO YOUR STOMACH?

CHOCOLATE-COVERED SNAILS.

WHY DID TAZ GO TO THE MOVIES?

HE WANTED TO PICK UP SOME
CHEWING GUM.

WHY DOES TAZ CATCH
CENTIPEDES?

HE LIKES BACON AND LEGS.

HE NEEDED DRESSING FOR HIS
POISON IVY SALAD.

WHAT DOES TAZ LIKE TO SPREAD ON HIS TOAST?

TOE JAM.

WHY DID TAZ INVITE SYLVESTER OVER FOR DINNER?

HE WANTED SOME SPAGHETTI AND HAIR BALLS.

WHAT'S WORSE THAN FINDING A DEAD WORM IN YOUR SPAGHETTI?

FINDING HALF A DEAD WORM.

WHY DID TAZ KEEP SWALLOWING LIVE FLIES?

BECAUSE HE HAD A FROG IN HIS THROAT.

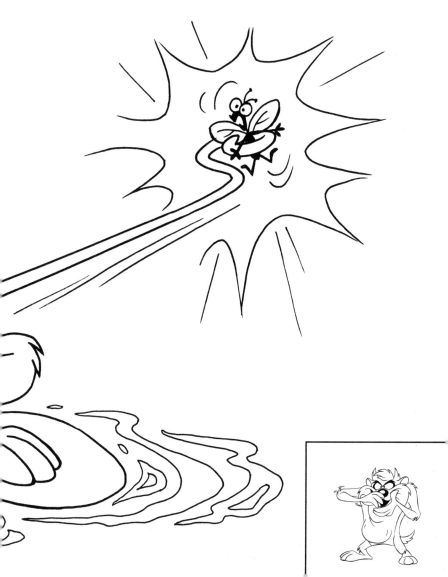

WHY DID TAZ WASH HIS FACE
WITH LAUNDRY STARCH?

HE WANTED TO KEEP A STIFF
UPPER LIP.

WHY DOES TAZ BITE HIS
FINGERNAILS?

BECAUSE HE CAN'T REACH HIS
TOENAILS.

WHAT DOES TAZ ORDER IN A CHINESE RESTAURANT?

SWEET AND SOUR PORKY.

WHAT DO YOU GET IF YOU CROSS A HYENA WITH A TASMANIAN DEVIL?

I DON'T KNOW. BUT IF HE LAUGHS, YOU'D BETTER JOIN IN.

WHY DID TAZ PUT AN OLD SHOE
IN HIS EAR?

HE LIKES TO LISTEN TO SOLE
MUSIC.

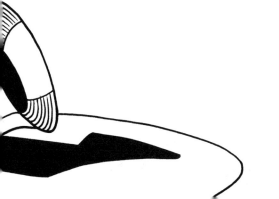

WHY DOESN'T TAZ LIKE CHEESE?

HE ALWAYS GETS HIS LIPS CAUGHT
IN THE MOUSETRAP.

WHAT IS TAZ'S FAVORITE DESSERT?

A LICE CREAM SODA.

WHY DID TAZ EAT A PACK OF NEEDLES AND A SPOOL OF THREAD?

BECAUSE HE WAS SEW HUNGRY.

WHAT DO YOU GET WHEN YOU
CROSS A CHICKEN WITH A
CENTIPEDE?

ENOUGH DRUMSTICKS FOR
EVERYBODY! (EVEN TAZ!)

WHAT DOES TAZ EAT FOR LUNCH WHEN HE HAS A COLD?

A SNEEZEBURGER AND A PIECE OF COUGHY CAKE FOR DESSERT.

WHAT DOES MICHIGAN J. FROG ORDER AT RESTAURANTS?

FRENCH FLIES.

WHY DID TAZ SHOVE
SNEAKERS UP HIS
NOSTRILS?

HE HAD A RUNNY NOSE.

WHAT DO YOU GET IF YOU CROSS TAZ WITH A PARROT?

I DON'T KNOW. BUT IF HE ASKS FOR A CRACKER, GIVE IT TO HIM!

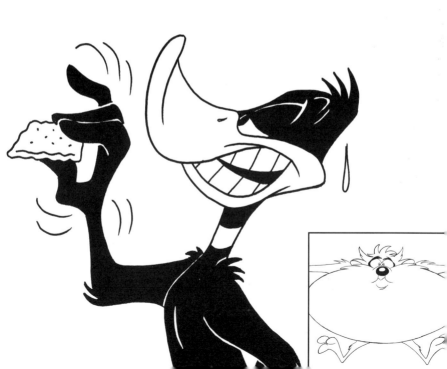

WHAT DO YOU CALL BUGS THAT CRAWL IN ONE EAR AND COME OUT THE OTHER?

IN-AND-OUT-SECTS.

WHY DID TAZ RUB A SKUNK
UNDER HIS ARMS?

HE WANTED TO SMELL GOOD FOR
HIS DATE.

HOW DID TAZ GET A STOMACH ACHE?

HE ATE SOMEONE WHO DISAGREED WITH HIM.

WHAT DO YOU GET WHEN YOU MIX LETTUCE, CUCUMBERS, AND FIVE HUNDRED DEAD FROGS?

A GREEN SALAD WITH THOUSAND EYE-LAND DRESSING.

WHAT SHOULD YOU DO IF ATTACKED BY THE TASMANIAN DEVIL?

SCREAM!!!

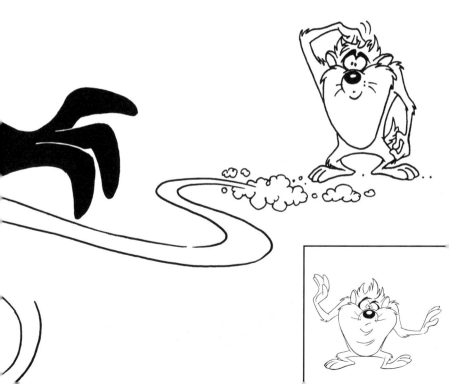

WHAT DOES TAZ EAT AT PARTIES?

BUTTERED HOST.

WHY DID TAZ BECOME A VEGETARIAN?

PEOPLE WERE TOO FATTENING.

WHAT'S WORSE THAN HAVING FIFTY DEAD EELS IN YOUR BED?

HAVING FIFTY LIVE EELS IN YOUR BED.

WHAT WAS THE FIRST THING TAZ DID AFTER HE WAS BORN?

HE ATE THE STORK.

WHY DID TAZ KISS A TOAD?

HE WANTED TO SEE HOW HE'D
LOOK WITH WARTS.

WHAT DID TAZ GET WHEN HE MIXED SLUGS WITH WATER AND ICE?

SLIME-ADE.

WHY DID TAZ WANT TO BECOME A
POLICE DETECTIVE?

SO HE COULD GRILL ALL THE
SUSPECTS.

WHAT DO YOU CALL A DENTIST WHO OFFERS TO CLEAN TAZ'S TEETH?

STUPID.

WHAT DID BUGS SAY WHEN TAZ
STARTED POURING ANTS ALL
OVER HIM?

"STOP BUGGING ME!"

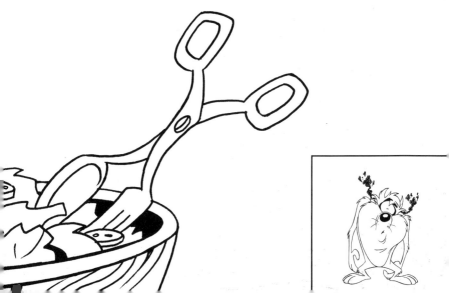

WHAT HAPPENED TO TAZ WHEN HE ATE A WINDOW?

HE HAD A PANE IN HIS STOMACH.

WHY DID TAZ GET CUT FROM THE BASKETBALL TEAM?

HE WAS DRIBBLING SO MUCH THAT HE FLOODED THE COURT.